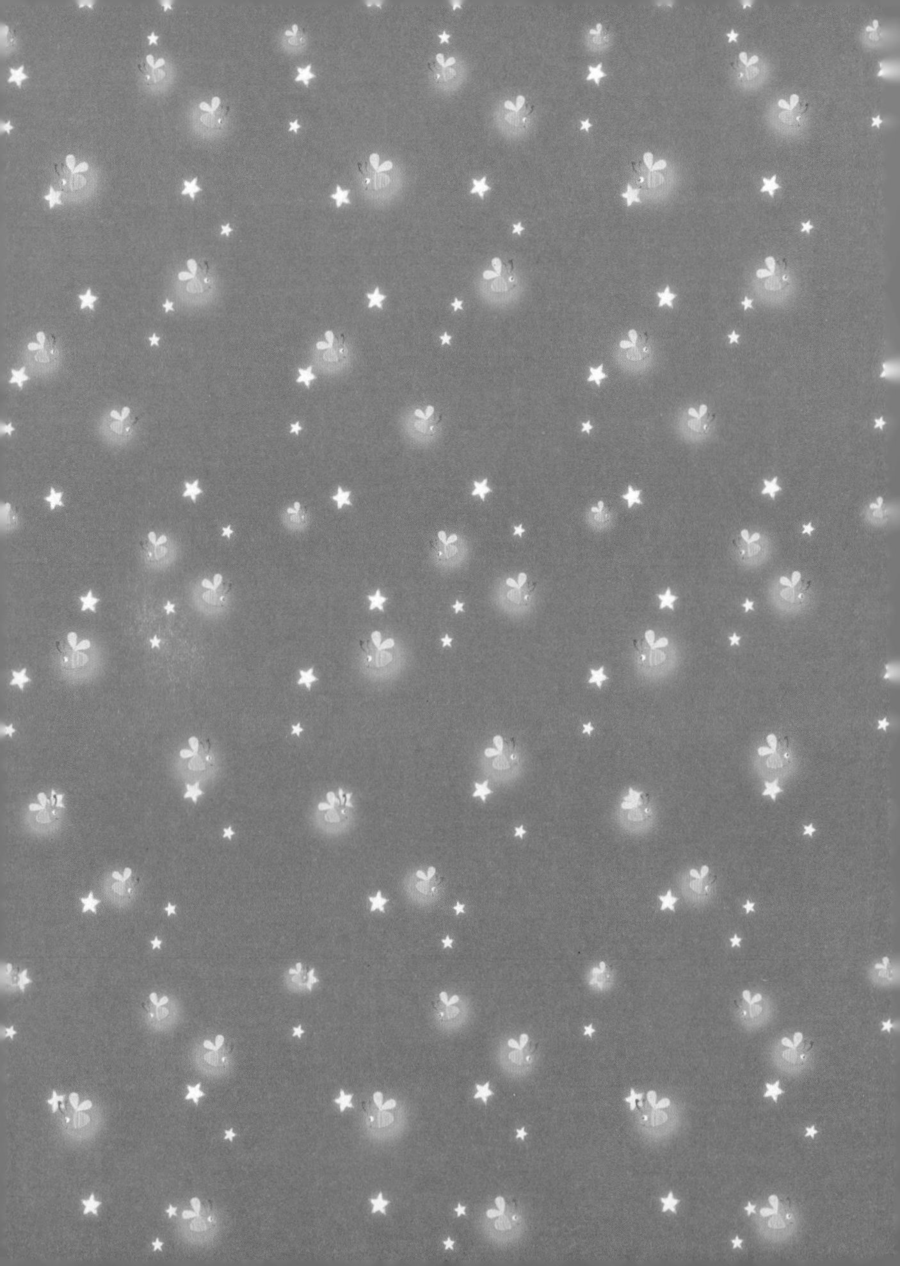

The Gingerbread Star

Anne Fine

With illustrations by Vicki Gausden

Barrington Stoke

First published in 2015 in Great Britain by
Barrington Stoke Ltd
18 Walker Street, Edinburgh, EH3 7LP

www.barringtonstoke.co.uk

This story was first published in a different form in
Read Me a Story Please (Orion Children's Books, 1998)

A CIP catalogue record for this book is available from the British Library upon request

ISBN: 978-1-78112-499-4

Printed in China by Leo

This book has dyslexia friendly features

For Theodore Boynton, with love

Contents

Chapter 1

Wonder

In an earthy burrow at the end of a very long lane lived a plain little grey worm. She was called Hetty. One evening, just before bedtime, Hetty saw a small light dancing in the dark wood.

It danced here. It danced there. It danced all over. The little glow shone in the shadowy places between the tall thin trees.

Hetty watched in wonder. “What is that little dancing light?” she asked her father.

"Why, that's a glow-worm," her father said. "It's called a glow-worm because it has a tiny light hidden inside its body."

"But I'm a worm too!" said Hetty. "And I don't glow! Why don't I have a little light inside my body?"

"Because you're just a plain grey worm," Hetty's mother said. "The sort of worm that can't fly. Glow-worms are different."

"Maybe I can't fly," Hetty said. "But I still wish I had a little glow of light inside my body."

"It's no use wishing that," her mother said.

Hetty said nothing. But she kept watching the lovely little light between the trees until it danced away.

Chapter 2

A Glow Inside

Next morning, Hetty woke up thinking about the glow-worm she had seen dancing between the trees. All day she wondered what it would be like to have a glow inside her.

She could light the way home through the woods when it was dark along the winding paths.

She could find all the odd little things that people had lost in shadowy corners.

Best of all, she could read in bed at night after dark, and no one would catch her.

Hetty longed to have a little light of her own, just like a glow-worm.

“Never mind,” her mother said.
“Come and have a cuddle.”

"Never mind," her father said. "Have a gingerbread star, fresh out of the oven."

But Hetty wasn't content with cuddles and gingerbread stars fresh out of the oven. Nice as those were, what she wanted was a light like a glow-worm.

She thought about it whenever she burrowed through the dark earthy tunnels under the ground.

She thought about it whenever she popped her head up to look at the fresh wet grass all around her.

She thought about it whenever she went to bed.

"Time for sleep," her father said. "Sweet dreams."

"No more reading," her mother warned.

But Hetty kept arguing with them. "If I was a glow-worm," she told them both, "then I could light the way home through the woods when it's dark. And I could find all the odd little things people have lost in shadowy corners. And I could keep reading my books under the covers at bedtime and no one would know."

Her mother and father laughed.

“That isn’t ever going to happen,” her father said.

“Not ever,” her mother agreed. “You’re just a plain grey worm and always will be.”

“You wait and see!” said Hetty. “Just you wait and see!”

Chapter 3

Gold Coins

When the sun rose in the morning, Hetty went up to the garden and sat on a flowerpot. She was busy thinking.

Maybe she could buy a little light to put inside her. But she would need a lot of money.

Who did she know who had a lot of money?

Of course! The rich man who lived in the grand house at the end of the lane.

So Hetty slid off the flowerpot and made her way down the garden path. She slid under the gate. She slid and slithered all the way along the grass until she reached the end of the lane.

She slid under the rich man's door and looked around.

There he was! He was sitting at a desk, taking his gold coins out of a bag and putting them in piles, to count them.

"Please," Hetty said. "Please can you give me enough money to buy a little light, so I can be like a glow-worm?"

The rich man looked up from his gold coins. He didn't seem at all surprised to see Hetty, but he did look curious.

“Why would a plain little grey worm like you want to be like a glow-worm?” he asked her.

Hetty explained. “Because then I can light the way home through the woods when it’s dark. And I’ll be able to find odd things that people have lost in shadowy corners. But, best of all, I will be able to read in bed at night and no one will catch me.”

The rich man laughed, then shook his head. “All the gold coins in the world can’t buy you a light like that,” he told Hetty. “Money doesn’t have that sort of power. I’m sorry, but you’ll have to find somebody else to help you.”

He went back to counting out his coins and very, very sadly Hetty went home.

"Never mind," said her mother. "Have a cuddle."

“Never mind,” said her father. “Have a gingerbread star.”

So Hetty had her cuddle and she ate her gingerbread star. But she wasn't happy. No, not at all. She still wanted to have a little light like a glow-worm hidden inside her body.

Chapter 4
The Queen

The next day, Hetty sat on her flowerpot and thought some more.

The rich man had said he couldn't buy her one of those wonderful glowing lights. He said that gold coins didn't have that sort of power.

So who did Hetty know who had a lot of power?

The Queen! The Queen must be the most powerful person in the land. Of course, the Queen could help her!

So Hetty slid off her flowerpot and slithered under the garden gate. She slithered all the way along to the Queen's palace.

She slid between the fancy palace gates and slithered all the way across the smooth green lawns until she saw the Queen.

The Queen was busy in a corner of her garden, gathering her favourite white roses to put in the palace bedrooms. Hetty slid closer.

"Please," Hetty said to the Queen. "Can you use your power to get me a little light inside my body, just like a glow-worm?"

The Queen put down her basket of beautiful white roses and looked at Hetty. “Why do you want to be a glow-worm?” she said. “Little grey worms like you are so useful in the garden.”

"Because then I'll be able to light the way home through the woods when it's dark," Hetty told her, "and find odd things that people have lost in shadowy corners. And, best of all, I will be able to read in secret in bed at night, and no one will catch me."

The Queen smiled and shook her head. "I'm sorry, Hetty. I can't help you. I do have power, yes. But it's not the sort of power that can get you a little glowing light inside your body. The kind of power you are looking for is magic power."

So very, very sadly Hetty had to turn around and slither home.

"Never mind," said her father. "Have a gingerbread star."

"Never mind," said her mother.
"Have a cuddle."

Hetty ate her gingerbread star. And she had her cuddle. But she still wasn't happy. No, not at all. She still wanted a little light inside her body, just like a glow-worm.

Chapter 5

Step After Step After Step

Next morning, even before Hetty had eaten her breakfast, she went up to sit on her flowerpot and think about where she could find some magic power.

"Who do I know who would have it?" she asked herself. And almost at once, the answer came to Hetty.

Of course! The wizard! The whole world knows that every wizard has a magic wand and a Big Book of Spells. Hetty would go and see the wizard.

So Hetty slid off her flowerpot and slithered all the way across the field.

She slithered under a gate and all the way up the steep hill to the wizard's tower.

She slid in under the door, and then she slid all the way up the winding stone steps.

The steps went round and round and up and up. Step after step after step, past all the doors to other rooms. As she climbed higher and higher, Hetty counted them.

Ninety-eight, ninety-nine ...

A hundred!

Hetty had reached the very top of the tower.

Hetty peeped in. There was the wizard. He was wearing a purple robe covered in beautiful gold stars. He had a pointy hat and a long white beard, and he looked just like all the wizards in the books that Hetty read at night.

The wizard didn't notice Hetty at first. He was too busy trying to make his cat Izzy come out of the corner. Izzy was his best helper and he needed her to help him with his spells.

But Izzy was in the most terrible mood because some of the wizard's early morning magic had gone wrong, and he had turned her paws bright pink and purple by mistake.

So Izzy sat in the corner in a great sulk. She wouldn't talk. She flicked her tail crossly and she didn't even turn around to look at Hetty as she slid into the room under the door.

Hetty was very polite, so she waited a long while before she spoke to the wizard. “Please,” she said at last. “I have come to ask if you would be kind and work one of your magic spells on me.”

The wizard didn't even ask Hetty what she wanted. "Sorry, but you'll have to wait," he said. "First, I must find my Big Book of Spells, so I can turn poor Izzy's paws back to jet black. Then maybe she'll stop sulking and start to help me again. After that, it will be your turn."

The wizard looked around, but his Big Book of Spells was nowhere to be seen.

The wizard sighed. “Drat!” he muttered to himself. “I must have left it somewhere in one of the ninety-nine other rooms.” He handed his magic wand to Hetty. “Hold this for me,” he said, “while I go down to find it.”

The wizard picked up Izzy and tucked her under his arm. Then he went off to try to find the Big Book of Spells in one of the ninety-nine other rooms of his tower.

Chapter 6

Real Gingerbread

Hetty was left all alone. She was alone for a very long time. It was cold at the top of the wizard's tower, and Hetty was bored. And, because she had left home before she had even had breakfast, Hetty was very, very hungry.

She looked at the star at the end of the wizard's magic wand. It was golden and glowing. Because Hetty was feeling so hungry, it reminded her of one her father's wonderful, freshly baked gingerbread stars – the kind he cooked whenever he was trying to cheer her up.

Hetty sniffed at the star on the end of the wizard's wand. To her surprise, it smelled all warm and spicy, just like one of her father's gingerbread stars.

She pressed it a little. It even felt like real gingerbread.

The wizard's star looked and felt exactly like one of her father's tasty gingerbread stars. And Hetty was horribly hungry. So, before she could stop herself, she had given the wizard's star a good long lick.

To her amazement, it even tasted like real gingerbread.

And all of a sudden, before she even realised what she was doing, Hetty had taken a little nibble. Then she took another, and another, and another, until she had eaten the whole star – yes, every last pointy bit of it.

Chapter 7

Poor Hetty

Poor Hetty was horrified. What had she done? The star had tasted wonderful. And she was no longer hungry. But Hetty knew she was in trouble now! Already she could hear the wizard coming back up the stairs to the tower room.

Now Hetty was only a plain little grey worm, but she was not stupid. She knew that if ever you swallow something odd, you have to tell, and you have to tell straight away.

So, when the wizard came back into the room with Izzy under one arm and his Big Book of Spells under the other, Hetty spoke up at once.

"Excuse me, Mr Wizard!" she said. "I gobbled up the star at the end of your magic wand by mistake."

The wizard wasn't listening. He was too busy looking round the tower room for the star that had vanished from the end of his wand.

"Please!" Hetty said, a bit louder. "I'm very sorry, but I have eaten the star off the end of your wand."

"Just a moment," said the wizard. "I cannot solve anybody's problems until I have found the star at the end of my wand."

Hetty burst into tears.

Chapter 8

Bliss!

The wizard just kept looking round the tower room for his magic wand. But as soon as Izzy the cat saw that Hetty was crying she stopped her sulking, and she told the wizard what had happened.

This time, the wizard listened.

He took the news quite well, considering it was his magic star that had been eaten.

"Thank you for telling me," he said to Hetty. "Or I might have spent hours and hours searching the ninety-nine other rooms for my missing star."

"It's always best to tell," Izzy agreed. "And there are plenty more wand stars in the cupboard. We bake them twice a week, and put the magic filling in on Thursdays."

"So," Hetty said, "I'm not poisoned?"

"Poisoned?" the wizard exclaimed. "Of course not! What a shocking idea! The very worst that will happen to you is that you'll start to glow a bit inside."

"Glow?" Hetty asked. All of a sudden she felt full of hope. "What? Like a real glow-worm?"

"I'm afraid so," said the wizard.

"How long will it last?" Hetty asked him.

"Until you grow up," the wizard said, "unless you are careless and leave it on all night."

"Oh, bliss!" said Hetty. "Oh, joy! The very thing I want!"

Cha

Everything

Hetty slithered round and round the room at the top of the tower in happy circles. She was waiting for the glow inside her to light up. The wizard watched her with a smile on his face. But Izzy was a bit more sensible.

[illegible]e’d better take Hetty home now,” [illegible]y said to the wizard. “It’ll be dark soon, and she’ll need time to learn how to turn on her light.”

“You’re right,” the wizard said. “Come on then. Let’s all go right now.”

The three of them set off together, step after step after step down the wizard’s tower, past all the other rooms.

Izzy was quite right. It was getting dark.

"Try the light now!" the wizard said to Hetty. "Think very hard, then whisper 'Magic, glow!' and the light should switch on."

Hetty stopped in her tracks. She coiled herself into a little grey circle and thought very hard indeed.

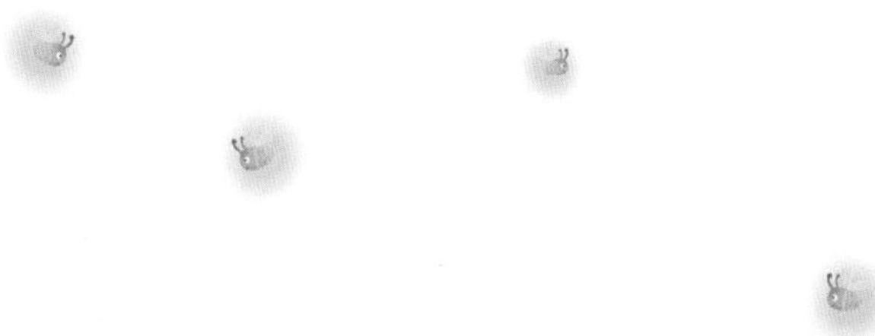

She whispered, “Magic, glow!” and saw a little light begin to shine about half way down her plain grey worm body.

“It works!” she said. “Oh, I am so excited because it works!”

The wizard stared at her. “Of course it works,” he said a little huffily. “When Izzy and I do magic, it always works.”

"Except when it doesn't," said Izzy, and she looked down at her paws, which were still pink and purple.

The wizard pretended that he hadn't heard what Izzy said. "Mostly it works," he said to Hetty. "And look! You can see for sure that it is working now."

And so it was. By the time the three of them reached the dark wood, Hetty was glowing as brightly as all the glow-worms dancing between the trees.

“Now try to switch it off,” the wizard said. “Think very hard and whisper to yourself, ‘Magic, stop!’”

Hetty soon learned to turn her little light on and off. All the way home, she practised till she had it pat.

On, off.

On, off.

“Well done!” the wizard said. “You’ve got it!”

“Yes,” Izzy agreed. “You’re doing very well.”

Just as they reached the garden gate, Hetty’s father popped his head out of the ground to call her in for supper.

“Goodbye,” the wizard said to Hetty. “It was so nice to meet you, even though I never did find out what spell it was you wanted.”

“I don’t want a spell any more,” said Hetty. “I have everything I want.”

“Good,” Izzy said, “because now the wizard and I can go home and turn my paws back to black.”

"Goodbye!" said Hetty. "And thank you!"

"It was a pleasure," said the wizard. And off he went with Izzy, back to the tower room to turn her paws back to black.

Chapter 10

In Bed

As the wizard and Izzy headed home, Hetty went down the wormhole for her tea.

"Good day?" her father asked her.

"Nice time?" asked her mother.

"Perfect!" said Hetty. "I am so happy. My wish came true and now I can do everything I wanted."

And so she could.

She could light the way home through the woods whenever it was dark.

She could find all the odd things that people had lost in shadowy corners.

Best of all, she could read in secret in bed at night and know that no one would catch her.

And since she was careful, and never left the little glow inside her on all night, it lasted till she was grown up.

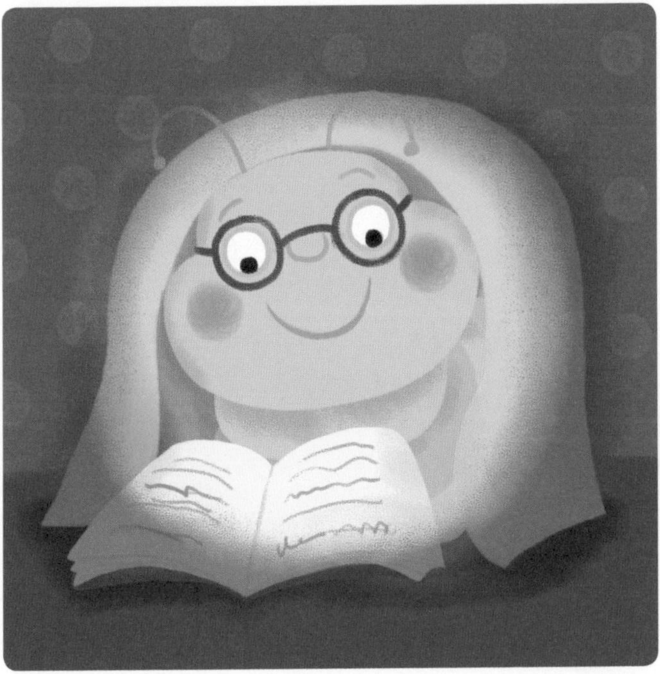

Our books are tested
for children and young people by
children and young people.

Thanks to everyone who consulted on
a manuscript for their time and effort in
helping us to make our books better
for our readers.

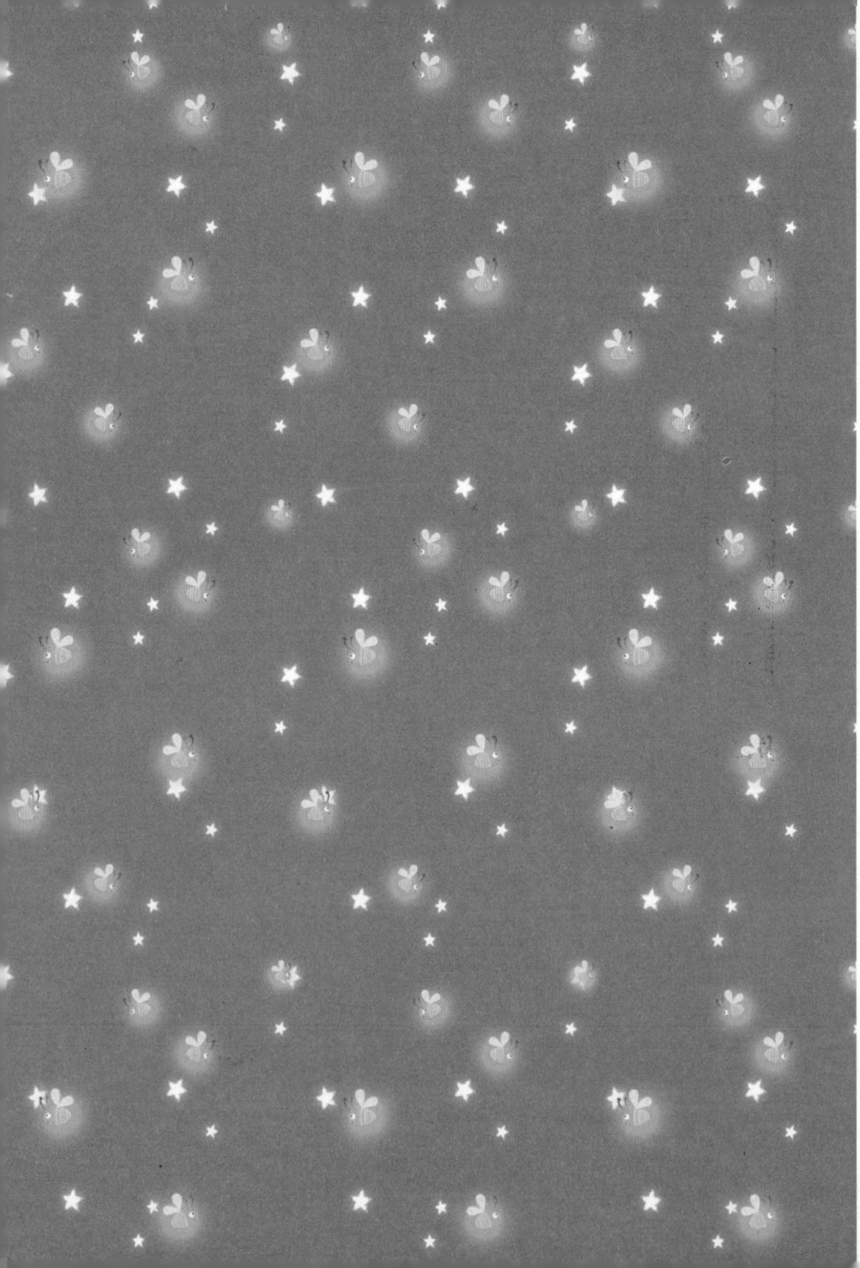